NO LONGER PROPERTY OF
SEATTLE PUBLIC LIBRARY

NO LONGER PROPERTY OF
SEATTLE PUBLIC LIBRARY

P9-BJE-980

2023

To: _____

From: _____

"Surely goodness and mercy shall follow
me all the days of my life: and I will dwell
in the house of the Lord forever."
—Psalm 23:6

Copyright © 2023 by Berenstain Publishing, Inc. All rights reserved. Published in the United States by
Random House Children's Books, a division of Penguin Random House LLC, New York. Random House and
the colophon are registered trademarks of Penguin Random House LLC.

Visit us on the Web!
rhcbooks.com
BerenstainBears.com

Educators and librarians, for a variety of teaching tools, visit us at RHTeachersLibrarians.com

Library of Congress Control Number: 2022933760
ISBN 978-0-593-30255-2 (trade) — ISBN 978-0-593-30527-0 (ebook)

MANUFACTURED IN CHINA
10 9 8 7 6 5 4 3 2 1

Random House Children's Books supports the First Amendment and celebrates the right to read.

Penguin Random House LLC supports copyright. Copyright fuels creativity, encourages diverse voices, promotes
free speech, and creates a vibrant culture. Thank you for buying an authorized edition of this book and for
complying with copyright laws by not reproducing, scanning, or distributing any part in any form without
permission. You are supporting writers and allowing Penguin Random House to publish books for every reader.

The Berenstain Bears
Gifts of the Spirit
Goodness

Mike Berenstain

Based on the characters created by
Stan and Jan Berenstain

Random House 🏠 **New York**

Something big was about to happen in Bear Country. It happened just once a year, so everyone looked forward to it. It was the rummage sale and country fair at the Chapel in the Woods! As always, the Bear family was in the thick of it, right up to their furry necks!

In fact, the whole neighborhood had been getting ready for months—sorting and tagging old clothes and home goods; getting the games, exhibits, and displays ready; and cooking and preparing all the good food that would be sold to raise money for the chapel.

Putting on a community event was not easy. Somebody had to be in charge, but not everyone wanted to do all the extra work. Mrs. Brown, the preacher's wife, always ended up with the job. Thankfully, she was cheerful and full of energy. What's more, she was patient and kind with everyone.

The cubs really liked Mrs. Brown. She ran the chapel's Sunday school and made everything fun and interesting.

When the day of the big event finally arrived, folks came streaming in from all over Bear Country. While parents shopped for bargains at the sale, the cubs had a fine old time at the fair.

There was the usual run of carnival games and other activities, like the beanbag toss, the ring-the-bell game, and a bouncy castle.

There was even a pony ride provided by Farmer Ben!

As a grand finale, Mrs. Brown had organized a parachute toss. Somehow, she'd managed to find a real parachute!

The cubs held the edges and tossed the center high in the air while they took turns running underneath as it floated down. There was something magical about being beneath that wavy parachute.

A wonderful time was had by all, and now it was time for the big community supper. Everyone marched to their places at the long picnic tables under the trees. They could smell the food cooking in the big outdoor kitchen. Yum!

Honey enjoyed everything at the fair. But most of all, she loved Mrs. Brown's parachute toss.

"You know," Honey said to Mama as they sat down to supper, "Mrs. Brown is a *genius*!"

Brother and Sister started to laugh. But Sister grew thoughtful. "Actually," she said, "Mrs. Brown *is* a genius. She's a genius at spreading *goodness*!"

Mama, Papa, and Brother had to agree. They didn't know anybody who was kinder or filled with more goodness than Mrs. Brown. Just then, Mrs. Brown came by to see how everyone was getting on.

"Mrs. Brown," asked Sister impulsively, "what do you think goodness is?"

"My, my, Sister!" laughed Mrs. Brown. "Such a serious question! But a serious question deserves a serious answer. My dear," she said, putting her hand on Sister's shoulder, "I believe that goodness comes from God, that God is love, and that the love of God passes all understanding."

Then Mrs. Brown gave Sister a big hug before going on her loving way.

"Whoa!" said Brother, impressed. "Heavy!"
"And beautiful!" added Mama, brushing away a tear.

Finally, it was time to say grace before the community meal. Everyone bowed their heads and joined hands as Preacher Brown led them in a prayer of thanksgiving for the blessings of love and fellowship. The Bear family smiled as their hearts were filled with goodness!

"And," Preacher Brown added, "the blessing of good food—let's eat!"

So they all dug in like a bunch of hungry bears.